Dear Baby
I'm Watching Over You

by Carol Casey · illustrated by Mark Braught

ISBN 978-0-9820972-3-6

Published by Dear Baby Books

www.dearbabybooks.com

Printed in the U.S.A. Publisher Control Number: MNWOU1010 First Printing

Distributed by National Book Network 1-800-462-6420

www.dearbabybooks.com

For inquiries to the Publisher, please email *info@dearbabybooks.com*

Dear Baby, I'm Watching Over You /

by Carol Casey; illustrated by Mark Braught

Summary: A tender letter from parents in the armed forces

to their children about all the ways they remain connected while apart

and why they choose to serve their country.

Written, illustrated, printed, and bound in the United States

Made In USA logo used with permission from Up-Ideas.com

Jacket & Book design by Up-Ideas.com

Dedications

- Carol Casey -
To U. S. service men, women, and veterans, and to your families.
Thank you for your patriotism and sacrifices,
and for watching over all of our children.

- Mark Braught -
For those that believe in, patriotically serve & sacrifice for
our way of life so we may enjoy the same.
Thank you.

Good morning, Baby.

On this brand new day,
I think of you and pray.
It's *my* way of watching over you.

Is Mama
reading you
my letter?
I hope my words
will help you
know me better.

They're my way
of watching over you.

I love how we traced
our hands together.

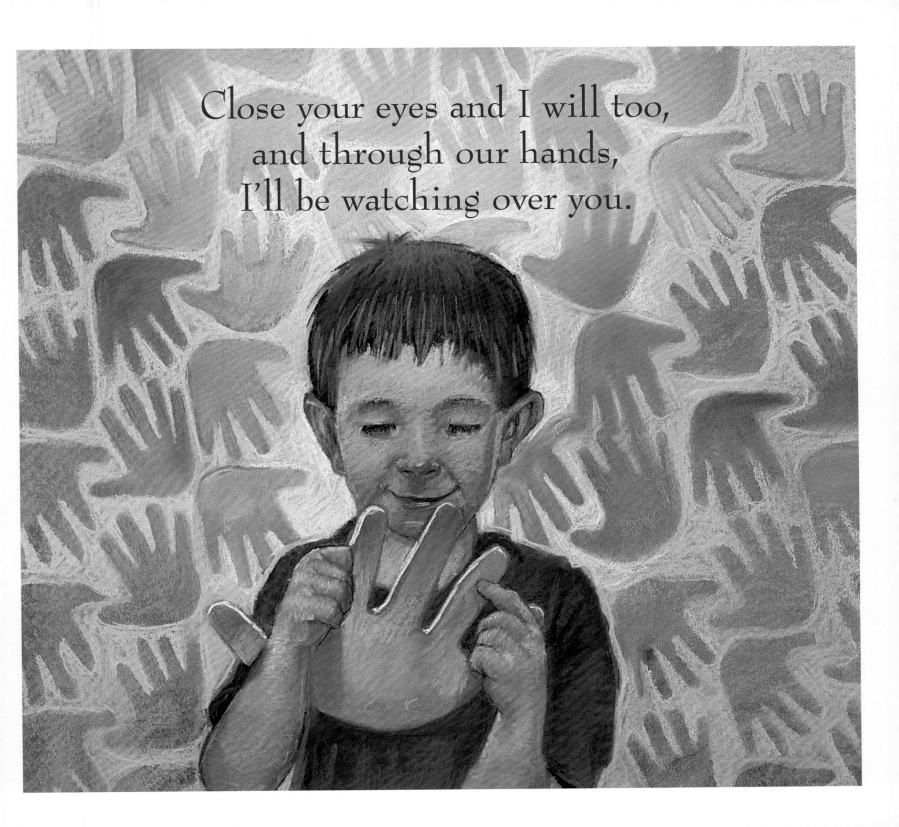

Close your eyes and I will too,
and through our hands,
I'll be watching over you.

You can see me
and I see you too.
It's my way
of watching over you.

It's just a little thing I do
so you'll know
I'm watching over you.

Thank you
for each picture and letter.
They really do make me feel better.

It also makes it clear to see
the caring way
you are watching over me.

I'm sure you wonder
why I'm away
for a birthday, game, or holiday.

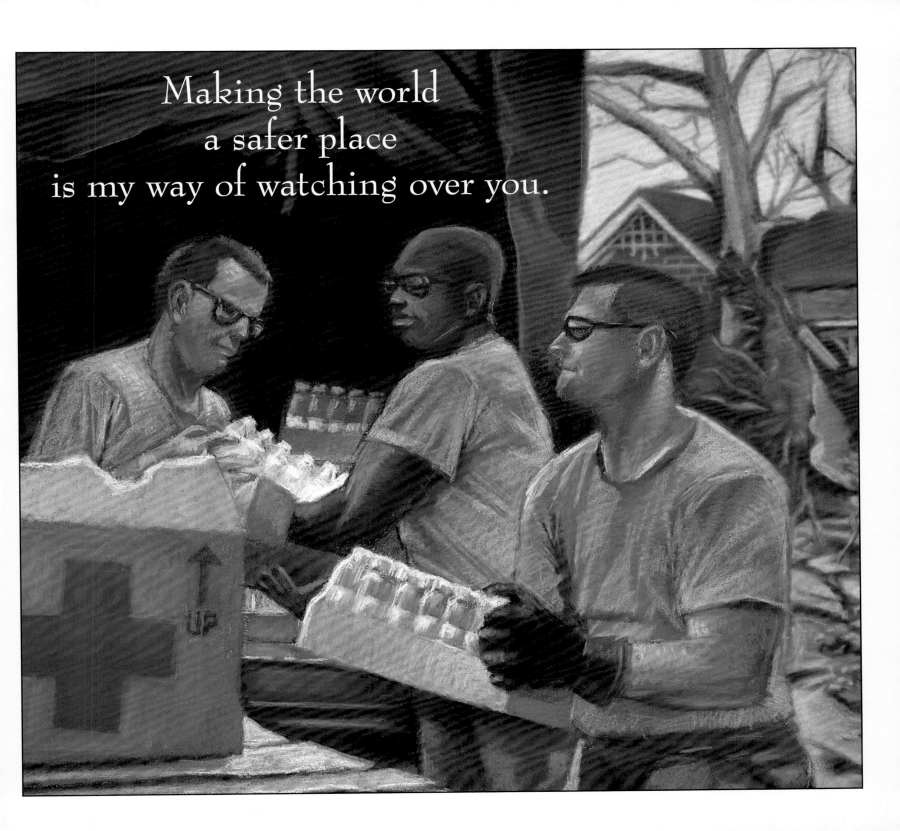

Making the world
a safer place
is my way of watching over you.

Honor, duty, freedom, and pride;
these are the reasons I decide
that protecting our country
is *my* way of watching over you.

There's so much about you
I've had to miss,

so I seal this letter
with a promise
and kiss.

In my deepest heart,
in my truest true,
I count the days
until I'm home
and I'm always,
always
watching over you.

Special acknowledgements:

To the soldiers and spouses I met along the way who shared their stories

To the staff and students and teachers at Fort Benning who gave us input and clarity on this story

To Duke Doubleday for his help in providing information and introductions

To Mark Braught for his beautiful paintings

To Editor Kara LaReau for her wise counsel

To my friend Heidi Salter for suggesting that I write a story for military families

And to my father Vincent Bicicchi, who served our country and taught me about patriotism

Published by Dear Baby Books

www.dearbabybooks.com   www.watchingoveryou.us

For inquiries to the Publisher, please email *info@dearbabybooks.com*

ROLL CALL
A record of who read this to you and with you.

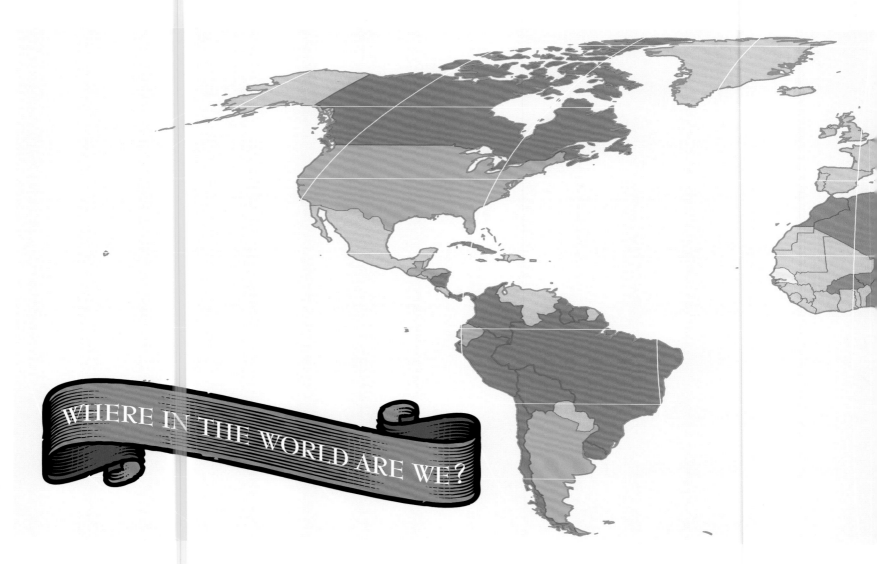

WHERE IN THE WORLD ARE WE?

Take a minute to find where you are on the map and mark it. Now find where your parent is in the world and mark that spot too!

Here you are (write the year and what country)

_____

_____

_____

_____

There they are (write the year and what country)

_____

_____

_____

_____

Other Dear Baby Books
for babies, toddlers, and pre-K kids

Dear Baby, It's a Colorful World
An endearing cast of multicultural toddlers,
cheerful rhymes, and vibrant landscapes
help young children learn
about the moods of colors,
while providing a gentle lesson on diversity.

Dear Baby, Let's Dance!
A joyful rhyming adventure
that introduces dance
in a comfortable family setting.

Dear Baby, What I love about you!
A wonderful first book for babies
that lets them know
why they are so irresistible.